PUFF

THE WORST WITCH
SPELLING BOOK

Jill Murphy started putting books together
(literally, with a stapler) when she was six.
Her *Worst Witch* series, the first of which was
published in 1975, is hugely successful. She has also
written and illustrated several award-winning
picture books for younger children.

By the same author

The Worst Witch
The Worst Witch Strikes Again
A Bad Spell for the Worst Witch
The Worst Witch All At Sea

THE
WORST WITCH'S
SPELLING
BOOK

JILL MURPHY
with Rose Griffiths

PUFFIN BOOKS

PUFFIN BOOKS

Published by the Penguin Group
Penguin Books Ltd, 27 Wrights Lane, London W8 5TZ, England
Penguin Books USA Inc., 375 Hudson Street, New York, New York 10014, USA
Penguin Books Canada Ltd, 10 Alcorn Avenue, Toronto, Ontario, Canada M4V 3B2
Penguin Books (NZ) Ltd, 182–190 Wairau Road, Auckland 10, New Zealand

Penguin Books Ltd, Registered Offices: Harmondsworth, Middlesex, England

First published 1995
5 7 9 10 8 6 4

Made and printed in England by Clays Ltd, St Ives plc

CONTENTS

Who's who
pages 6 and 7

Spelling checks and word puzzles
pages 8 to 71

Answers
pages 72 to 80

PUPILS

This is Miss Cackle's Academy for Witches where Mildred and Maud go to school.

This is Mildred, the worst witch in the school.

This is her friend Maud.

This is Tabby, Mildred's cat.

TEACHERS

Miss Cackle and Miss Hardbroom
are two of the teachers.

This is
Miss Hardbroom.

This is
Miss Cackle.

SPELLING CHECKS

Test your spelling!
Use a Check Slip to help you.

These are
the words
I want to
practise...

frog

kitten

kipper

I study the words, cover
them up with a piece of
paper, and write down
the words to test myself.

Did I get them right?

Yes/No

frog

frog
kitten
kipper

frog
kitten
kipper

Make a Check Slip to test yourself on
these words.

Read each word	Cover it up	Write it down	Uncover it to check it.

	frog
	kitten
	kipper
	spider
	beetle
	monkey
	mouse
	snail

Practise any words you get wrong, then
test yourself again.

CAT IN MOTION

How is Tabby travelling?

Put these words in the right places:

broomstick   **basket**   **satchel**

1.

satchel

2.

basket

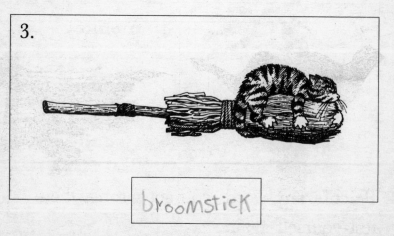

3.

broomstick

WITCH IN MOTION

How is Mildred moving?
Put these words in the right places:

flying   falling   walking   skipping

1. skipping

2. walking

3. falling

4. flying

WORDS WITH TWO T'S

There are two T's
in the middle of

K	I	T	T	E	N

What are these words?

1. 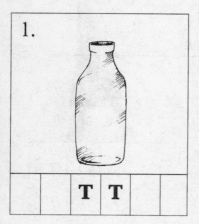	2. 
		T	**T**						**T**	**T**		
3. 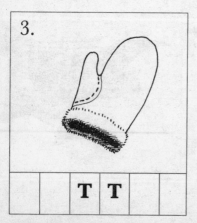	4. 
		T	**T**						**T**	**T**		

DAYTIME

Finish the labels on Mildred.

hat

b a t

plait

p l a i t

pyjamas

cloak

sock

broomstick

b o o t

boot

cat

Now try the labels on the next page.

NIGHT TIME

Look back to the page before, to check your spelling!

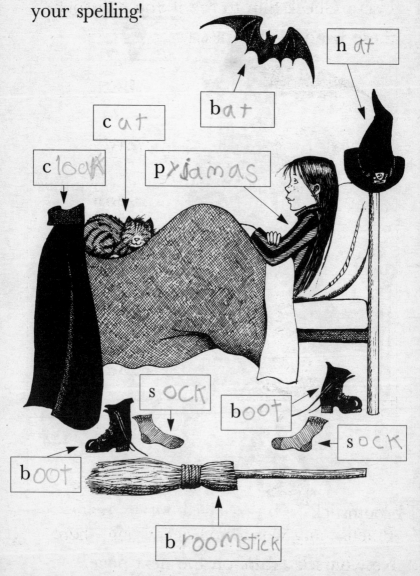

h at

b a t

c at

c l o a k

p y j a m a s

s o c k

b o o t

s o c k

b o o t

b r o o m s t i c k

14

NIGHT WORDS
SPELLING CHECK

Use a Check Slip to see if you can spell these words (see pages 8 and 9).

	bat
	owl
	moon
	stars
	cloud
	candle
	midnight
	silhouette

Practise any words you get wrong, then test yourself again.

BREAKFAST

Decide which word to put in each place.

porridge   toast   cornflakes   kippers

1.

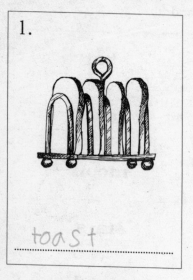

toast

2. Where have
   they all gone?

kippers

3.

It's
atrocious!

porridge

4. They're
   crunchy!

cornflakes

16

Now put these words in the right places:

marmalade kippers porridge toast

I *love* fish!

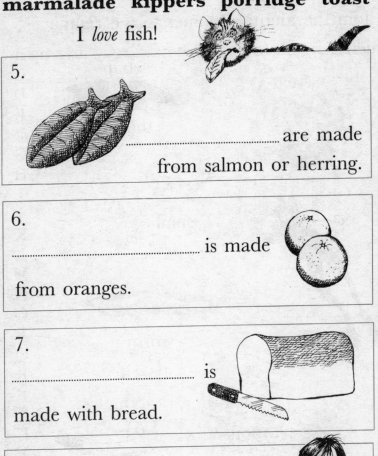

5. .... are made
from salmon or herring.

6. .... is made
from oranges.

7. .... is
made with bread.

8. ....
is made with oats.
I like it!

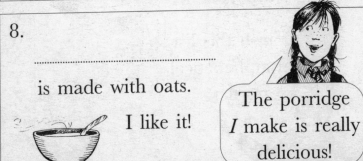

The porridge *I* make is really delicious!

ALPHABETICAL ANIMALS

Join the animals' names to the right letter in the alphabet.

cat

bat

snail

frog

worm

mouse

A B C D E F G H I J K L M N O P Q R S T U V W X Y Z

bat
....
....
....
....
....

Finish this list in alphabetical order.

COLOURS

What colours do you like?

Black, red, blue, yellow, green, orange, pink, grey, brown and white.

Nine of these colours are hidden here.
Can you find them?

A	G	R	E	E	N	C	J	E	I	G
O	B	D	B	L	A	C	K	F	H	B
R	N	O	M	S	R	V	Q	L	T	L
A	Y	E	L	L	O	W	P	U	K	U
N	W	X	A	C	P	Z	D	F	G	E
G	R	E	Y	B	I	Y	R	E	D	E
E	H	J	P	I	N	Q	S	M	Z	L
K	G	R	O	W	K	W	H	I	T	E

Which colour is missing?

....

RIGHT AND LEFT

I'm holding out my **right** arm.

Which arm are we holding out in each picture?
Put **right** or **left**.

1.

2.

3.
....

4.
....

5.
....

COLOURS CROSSWORD

Remember . . .
Write your answers in
CAPITAL letters.

CLUES:

1 down:
I am this colour.

3 down:
The colour
of my hat.

4 down:
The colour of tomatoes.

7 down:
The colour
of snow.

2 across:
The background
colour
of school
badge.

5 across:
The colour of the sky on a sunny day.

6 across:
The colour of a candle flame.

8 across:
The colour of a kitten's tongue.

9 across:
The colour of carrots.

SILHOUETTES

This is Mildred's silhouette.

A silhouette is the dark
shape of something.

Some people can make pictures
of people they know, by cutting shapes
out of black paper.

One man, who lived in France a long
time ago, was famous for doing this.
His name was Etienne de Silhouette, and
the shapes were called "silhouettes" after
him. Jill Murphy likes to make a silhouette
by drawing a black outline and then filling
it in.

Fill in the missing letters:

sil	hou	ette		silhou	ette
sil					ette
sil		ette		s	

Which silhouette is which?
One is Tabby, one is Miss Hardbroom,
and one is Maud.

| ....'s | ....'s | ....'s |
| **silhouette** | **silhouette** | **silhouette** |

Finish writing these:

silhou ....

s ....

A mouse's

s ....

"ING" WORDS

Use these words to fill the spaces:

**lacing   swimming   purring   flying
drinking   sleeping   running**

1.
Ethel is

....

beautifully.

2.

.... is faster

than walking.

3.
Doing up your boots
is called

...............................them.

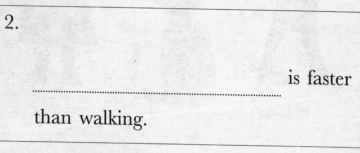

4.

When Tabby is happy
you can hear him

....

5. Miss
    Hardbroom is

....

6. Miss
    Hardbroom is

....

7.

Moving your arms
and legs to go through
water is called

....

TAPE A TEST

When I write a letter or a story, there are some words I nearly always spell wrongly.

These are the words I need to practise!

Sometimes I help Mildred learn her spellings.

We make a list of four or five words. I read out each word, then say it again in a sentence.

You could make a tape, to help you test yourself.

Tick the box if you have
a cassette recorder and a tape to use:

You could say something like this on your tape:

"Here is my spelling test for this week. Five words to test!

1. **know**   Do you know who I am?

2. **friend**   Emma is my friend.

3. **because** I like Maud because she makes me laugh.

4. **please**   May I have an apple, please?

5. **said**   Mildred said, 'Hello.'

Now switch off and check them!"

Do your test once or twice a day, and practise in between with a Check Slip

(see pages 8 and 9).

HUNDREDS

Join a word to its meaning with a line.

centipede

century

cent

1. A hundred years

How long has this tree been growing?

2. A little animal

Has it got a hundred legs?

3. Money

There are a hundred cents in a dollar.

What do you think "cent" means?

HOW OLD ARE YOU?

In which month were you born? ....

In which year were you born? ....

How old are you? ....

> * A **fortnight** is two weeks...fourteen
> nights.
> * A **decade** is ten years.
> * A **century** is a hundred years.

Are you more than a decade old? **Yes/No**

How old is each person in these photos?
Write | **fortnight** | **decade** | or | **century** | !

1. ....

2. ....

3. ....

ANIMALS CROSSWORD

Remember to write your answers in CAPITAL letters.

CLUES:

1 across:

4 across: Enid's pet.

7 across:

Mildred turned Ethel into a ....

8 across:

What did Mildred say was under her bed, to trick Griselda?

 *or*

9 across:

I'm Agatha Cackle!

Mildred turned her into a

....

2 down:
Who is this?

3 down:
Ethel turned Mildred into a ....

5 down: Mildred smelt fishy when she took these for Tabby's breakfast.

6 down: These were a problem in the kitchen.

WHAT'S MISSING?

ABCDEFGHIJKLNOPQRSTUVWXYZ

This alphabet has one letter missing...

It's M!

Find the missing letter from each alphabet.
Write it in the box.

ABCDEFGHIJKLNOPQRSTUVWXYZ	
ABCDEFGHIJKLMNPQRSTUVWXYZ	
ABCDEFGHIJKLMOPQRSTUVWXYZ	
ABCDEFGHIJLMNOPQRSTUVWXYZ	
ABCDFGHIJKLMNOPQRSTUVWXYZ	
ABCDEFGHIJKLMNOPQRSTUVWXZ	

I changed my cat into a ☐☐☐☐☐☐!

"DIS" WORDS

disappeared   disappointed

How many **s** s are there
in each word?

How many **p** s are there
in each word?

Fill in "disappeared" or "disappointed":

1. Mildred and Maud

....

when they made
the wrong potion.

2. Miss Cackle was

....

because Mildred kept
getting into trouble.

MIXED-UP NAMES

Sort out these mixed-up names.

3.

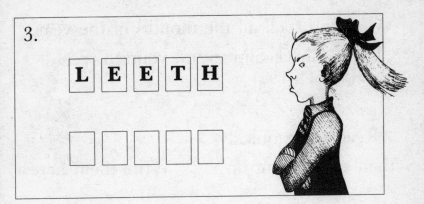

| L | E | E | T | H |

| | | | | |

4.

Mildred kidnapped her!

| D | E | S | G | R | I | L | A |

| | | | | | | | |

5.

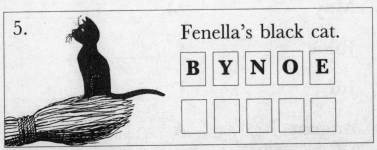

Fenella's black cat.

| B | Y | N | O | E |

| | | | | |

MONTHS

Can you spell all the months of the year?
Use a Check Slip to test yourself
(see pages 8 and 9).

Read these quickly
then cover them up...

Write them here:

January	J ....
February	F ....
March	M ....
April	A ....

Now try these...

May	M ....
June	J ....
July	J ....
August	A ....

Now try these... Write them here:

September	S_____
October	O_____
November	N_____
December	D_____

It will take me *all year* to learn these!

Don't worry. Just learn a few at a time.

The puzzles on the next two pages will help you.

MORE MONTHS

January	May	September
February	June	October
March	July	November
April	August	December

Eleven months are hidden here.
Can you find them?

```
B A A U G U S T J C S
J K G F D I H J U N E
D E C E M B E R L O P
R S P J M L N Q Y V T
F A C A P R I L T E E
G X B N E D H J U M M
T K Y U W V M B O B B
S Z M A N R A Q P E E
F E B R U A R Y W R R
U M A Y B D C I F V I
L N Y Z P R H X G J K
```

Which month is missing? ....

40

Look for patterns to help you remem**ber** ...

Which months have **uary** at the end?

....

Which months have **ber** at the end?

....

....

Which months have **u** as the second letter?

....

....

CAT WORDS

It smells wonderful!

Catmint

is a plant
which cats like.

What are these "cat words"?

1.

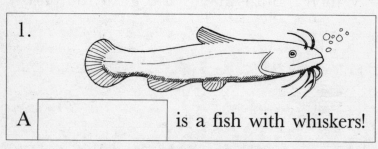

A ☐ is a fish with whiskers!

2.

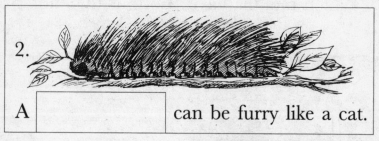

A ☐ can be furry like a cat.

3.

ZZZZ

A ☐ is a little sleep.

Some words which begin with "cat" have nothing to do with cats!

Put these words in the right places:

catastrophe   **catamaran**   **catapult**

4.

5.

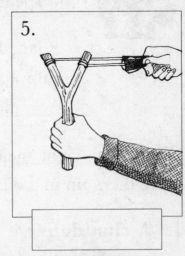

6.

WHICH MEANING?

Are you looking up a spell?

No, I'm looking up a word in my dictionary.

Choose the right meaning for each word.
Look them up in a dictionary if you want to.

1. A **chandelier** is...

    a. a cold drink
    b. a kind of light
    c. a dance

Put the right letter in the box.

2. A **catastrophe** is...

   a. a basket for a cat
   b. a sailing boat
   c. a terrible disaster

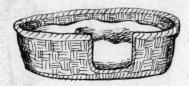

3. If you are **yowling**, you are...

   a. painting things yellow
   b. making a horrible noise
   c. running as fast as you can

4. A **legend** is...

   a. a small shelf
   b. a wooden box
   c. an old story

HIDDEN WORDS

Look at each picture.

Write each word in the spaces across.

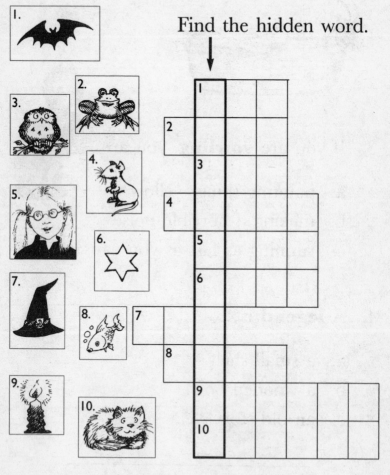

Find the hidden word.

What is the hidden word?

....

46

Now try this puzzle!

Find the hidden word.

1							
	2						
3							
	4						
		5					
6							
7							

What is the hidden word?

....

ODD ONES OUT

Which of these words
is the odd one out:
tea, orange, toast or milk?

It's toast, because
you can't drink it!

Find each odd one out. Why is it odd?

1.

| Ebony | Tabby | Ethel | Night Star |

The odd one out is ....

because ....

....

2. | cloudy | silly | sunny | rainy |

The odd one out is ....

because ....

....

3.

| bucket | jug | bowl | blanket |

The odd one out is ....

because ....

....

4. | crumpets | stones | buns | toast |

The odd one out is ....

because ....

....

TIME WORDS

Choose the right meaning for each word.
Write a, b or c in each box.

1. A **decade** is...
   a. five years
   b. ten years
   c. twenty years

   [ ]

   I've been a frog
   for decades.

2. A **century** is...
   a. ten years
   b. fifty years
   c. a hundred years

   [ ]

   This castle is
   centuries old!

3. A **week** is...
   a. five days
   b. seven days
   c. nine days

   [ ]

Are we going on holiday for a week or a fortnight?

4. A **fortnight** is…
   a. two days
   b. two weeks
   c. two years

5. In every **year**, there are…
   a. eight months
   b. ten months
   c. twelve months

6. February is the name of…
   a. a month
   b. a day
   c. a season

MILDRED'S CROSSWORD

Write your answers on the crossword in CAPITAL letters.

CLUES:

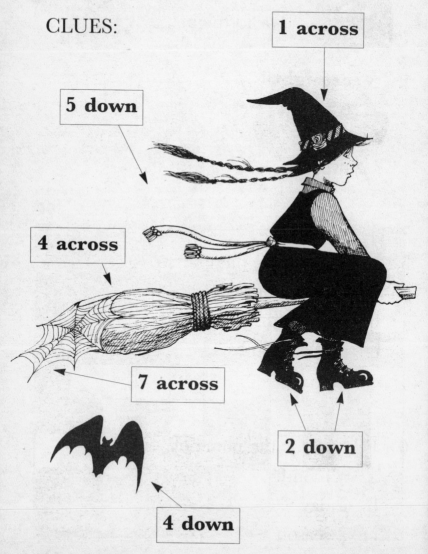

1 across

5 down

4 across

7 across

2 down

4 down

1 down: The 31st of October is called

H ....

3 across:

6 across:

53

MORE MEANINGS

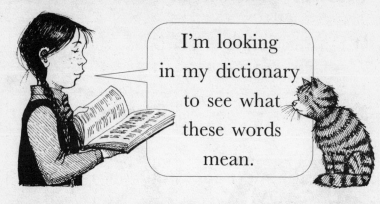

I'm looking in my dictionary to see what these words mean.

Choose the right meaning for each word.
Write a, b or c in each box.

That dress is too frivolous.

1. **Frivolous** means…
   a. fruity
   b. silly, not serious
   c. very colourful

2. A **crevice** is…

    a. a narrow crack

    b. a crispy biscuit

    c. a beetle

3. If you are **staggering**, you are…

    a. singing a song as you walk along

    b. nearly falling over when you walk

    c. jumping over rocks

4. A **dormitory** is…

    a. a tiny mouse

    b. a camel

    c. a place to sleep

SEASONS

Our school is cold and damp all year...spring, summer, autumn and winter!

I think **autumn** is the hardest season to spell!

Fill in the missing letters:

autumn

aut _____

_____ tumn

autu _____

_____

A					
	U	T	U		
	U		U		
		T			
				M	N

Which season is it, in each picture?

1.

2.

3.

4.

MORSE CODE

Why are you flashing that torch?

I'm sending a message to Enid in Morse code.

Over 150 years ago, a man called Samuel Morse invented a way of sending messages using electricity. He made up a code of dots and dashes.

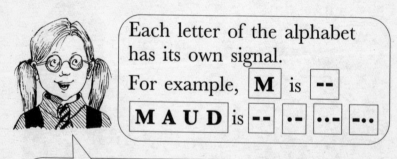

Each letter of the alphabet has its own signal.

For example, **M** is **--**

M A U D is **--** **·-** **··-** **-··**

You can send messages with short and long flashes on a torch, or with short and long blows on a whistle.

The shortest signal you can do is just one dot. It stands for the letter we use most often.

Which *do* we use most often?

Count up how many times each letter is used in this message:

I LIKE SENDING A MORSE MESSAGE INSTEAD OF WRITING A LETTER

A	J	S
B	K	T
C	L	U
D	M	V
E	N	W
F	O	X
G	P	Y
H	Q	Z
I	R	

Which letter is used the most? ☐ is ☐•

Fill in the rest of the code for Mildred:

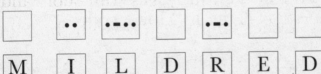

| ☐ | •• | •–•• | ☐ | •–• | ☐ | ☐ |
| M | I | L | D | R | E | D |

MORE MORSE

Here are all the letters in the Morse code:

A	B	C	D	E	F	G	H	I
.-	-...	-.-.	-..	.	..-.	--.	....	..

J	K	L	M	N	O	P	Q
.---	-.-	.-..	--	-.	---	.--.	--.-

R	S	T	U	V	W	X	Y	Z
.-.	...	-	..-	...-	.--	-..-	-.--	--..

.	-.	..	-..

Write *your* name in Morse code:

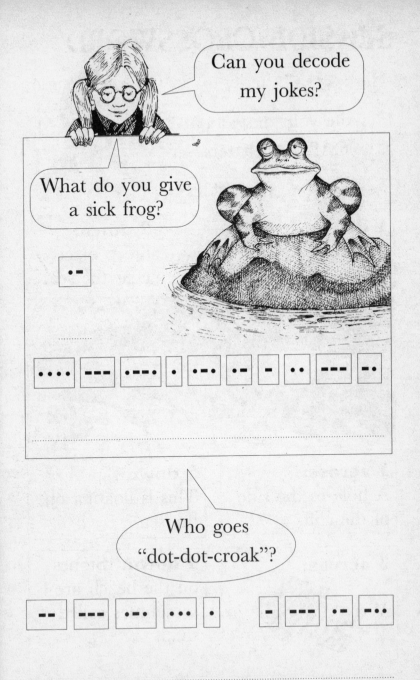

61

SEASIDE CROSSWORD

Remember to write your answers in CAPITAL letters.

CLUES:

1 down: Mildred and Form 2 stayed in a ...... at the seaside.

2 down: Steep place near the sea.

1 across: A hole in the side of the cliff.

5 down: This is floating on the sea.

3 across:

4 down: Stones on the beach are sometimes called sh.....

5 across:

The shore of the sea, made of sand or pebbles.

6 across:

7 across:

ALPHABETICAL NAMES

Put our names in alphabetical order

Ethel

Sybil

Clarice

Who comes first out of Ethel and me? We both begin with **E**!

Enid

Mildred

Maud

Look at your second letters. N comes before T, so **E<u>n</u>id** comes before **E<u>t</u>hel**.

CL

Finish this list.

A B C D E F G H I
J K L M N O P Q R
S T U V W X Y Z

"SCOPE" WORDS

Draw lines to show what you can see with each "scope".

telescope

1.

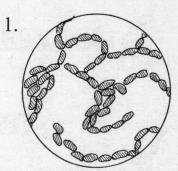

kaleidoscope

2.

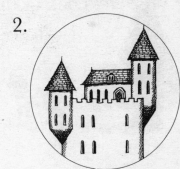

microscope

3.

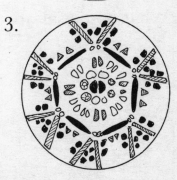

What do you think "scope" means?

BRIGHT NIGHT

It's a **bright** **night**!

This bag is very **light**

My bag is quite a **weight**

Look at those bats! I can see **eight**

What is special about the words like **this** ?

These words have **g** **h** **t** in them.
What are they?

1. How many legs have I got?

E ☐ ☐ ☐ ☐

2. N ☐ ☐ ☐ ☐

D ☐ ☐ ☐ ☐ ☐ ☐ ☐
3. Hello, Mum!

4. A hundred and fifty centimetres

H ☐ ☐ ☐ ☐ ☐

Practise your spelling on the next two
pages...

67

EIGHT WORDS

Hello, Enid!

I **thought** you'd forgotten me!

We're going to practise these **eight** words.

That's not **right!** There are **ten** words!

These five words rhyme. Use a Check Slip to test yourself

(see pages 8 and 9).

bright
fright
light
night
right

These two words look similar but they sound quite different!

weight　　　**height**

Cover them up and write them here:

....　...................................

Fill in the missing letters for these three words:

daughter

dau...................

d.....**ghter**

daugh...............

d...................

thought

thou...........

t...................

eight

ei...........

e...........

69

WORD QUIZ

Try my word quiz.
Write a, b, c or d in
each box.

1. Which of these is the shortest?

a. **a decade**   c. **a day**

b. **a minute**   d. **a week**

2. Which of these months is in the summer?

a. **January**   c. **August**

b. **April**   d. **December**

3. Which animal is the odd one out?

a. **bat**   c. **owl**
b. **seagull**   d. **spider**

4. Which word means "disappeared"?

a. **finished**   c. **varnished**
b. **vanished**   d. **polished**

5. What is the opposite of "first"?

a. **end**   c. **finish**
b. **start**   d. **last**

This is our last puzzle!
The answers are on
the next few pages.

ANSWERS

CAT IN MOTION *(page 10)*

1. satchel　2. basket　3. broomstick

WITCH IN MOTION *(page 11)*

1. skipping　2. walking　3. falling
4. flying

WORDS WITH TWO T'S *(page 12)*

1. BOTTLE　2. KETTLE　3. MITTEN
4. LITTER

BREAKFAST *(pages 16 and 17)*

1. toast　2. kippers　3. porridge
4. cornflakes　5. kippers　6. marmalade
7. toast　8. porridge

ALPHABETICAL ANIMALS *(page 18)*

bat
cat
frog
mouse
snail
worm

COLOURS *(page 19)*

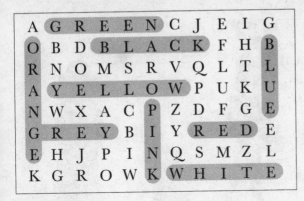

Which colour is missing? **BROWN**

RIGHT AND LEFT *(pages 20 and 21)*

1. left 2. right 3. right 4. right 5. left

COLOURS CROSSWORD *(pages 22 and 23)*

SILHOUETTES *(pages 24 and 25)*

Miss Hardbroom's silhouette

Maud's silhouette

Tabby's silhouette

"ING" WORDS *(pages 26 and 27)*

1. flying 2. running (or flying!) 3. lacing
4. purring 5. drinking 6. sleeping
7. swimming

HUNDREDS *(page 30)*

1. century   2. centipede   3. cent

"cent" means **"a hundred"**

HOW OLD ARE YOU? *(page 31)*

1. fortnight (two weeks)
2. century (a hundred years)
3. decade (ten years)

74

ANIMALS CROSSWORD (*pages 32 and 33*)

WHAT'S MISSING? (*page 34*)
  MONKEY

"DIS" WORDS (*page 35*)
1. disappeared 2. disappointed

MIXED-UP NAMES (*pages 36 and 37*)
1. TABBY 2. MILDRED 3. ETHEL
4. GRISELDA 5. EBONY

MORE MONTHS *(pages 40 and 41)*

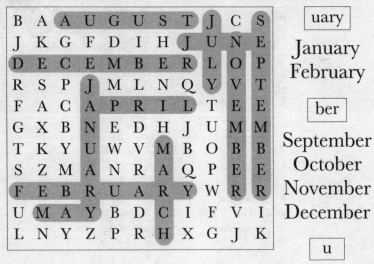

B	A	U	G	U	S	T	J	C	S
J	K	G	F	D	I	H	U	N	E
D	E	C	E	M	B	E	R	L	O	P
R	S	P	J	M	L	N	Q	Y	V	T
F	A	C	A	P	R	I	L	T	E	E
G	X	B	N	E	D	H	J	U	M	M
T	K	Y	U	W	V	M	B	O	B	B
S	Z	M	A	N	R	A	Q	P	E	E
F	E	B	R	U	A	R	Y	W	R	R
U	M	A	Y	B	D	C	I	F	V	I
L	N	Y	Z	P	R	H	X	G	J	K

uary

January
February

ber

September
October
November
December

u

June July
August

Which month was missing?
OCTOBER

CAT WORDS *(pages 42 and 43)*
1. catfish 2. caterpillar 3. catnap
4. catamaran 5. catapult 6. catastrophe

WHICH MEANING? *(pages 44 and 45)*

1. b   2. c   3. b   4. c

HIDDEN WORDS *(pages 46 and 47)*

	¹B	A	T
²F	R	O	G
	³O	W	L
⁴M	O	U	S	E
	⁵M	A	U	D
	⁶S	T	A	R
⁷H	A	T
	⁸F	I	S	H
	⁹C	A	N	D	L	E
	¹⁰K	I	T	T	E	N

B R O O M S T I C K
S N A I L
C A S T L E
S P I D E R
W O R M
B U C K E T
C A U L D R O N

Mildred!

Broomstick!

ODD ONES OUT *(pages 48 and 49)*

1. Ethel, because she is not a cat.
2. silly, because the others are to do with the weather.
3. blanket, because you cannot keep water in it.
4. stones, because you cannot eat them.

TIME WORDS *(pages 50 and 51)*

1. b   2. c   3. b   4. b   5. c   6. a

MILDRED'S CROSSWORD *(pages 52 and 53)*

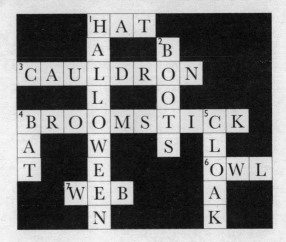

MORE MEANINGS *(pages 54 and 55)*

1. b   2. a   3. b   4. c

SEASONS *(pages 56 and 57)*

1. summer   2. autumn

3. spring   4. winter

MORSE CODE *(pages 58 and 59)*

The letter which is used the most is E.

"Mildred" is

MORE MORSE *(pages 60 and 61)*

ENID is behind the wall!

What do you give a sick frog?

A HOPERATION

Who goes "dot-dot-croak"?

MORSE TOAD

SEASIDE CROSSWORD *(pages 62 and 63)*

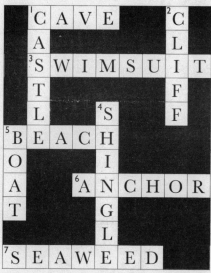

	1 C	A	V	E			2 C	
	A						L	
	3 S	W	I	M	S	U	I	T
	T						F	
	L			4 S			F	
5 B	E	A	C	H				
O				I				
A			6 A	N	C	H	O	R
T				G				
				L				
7 S	E	A	W	E	E	D		

ALPHABETICAL NAMES *(page 64)*

Clarice
Enid
Ethel
Maud
Mildred
Sybil

"SCOPE" WORDS *(page 65)*

1. microscope
2. telescope
3. kaleidoscope

"scope" is from the Greek word which means "I see".

BRIGHT NIGHT *(pages 66 and 67)*

All the words have **ght** in them.

1. EIGHT   2. NIGHT
3. DAUGHTER   4. HEIGHT

WORD QUIZ *(pages 70 and 71)*

1. b   2. c   3. d   4. b   5. d

Goodbye!